Other books by Mick Inkpen

KIPPER

ONE BEAR AT BEDTIME

THE BLUE BALLOON

THREADBEAR

BILLY'S BEETLE

KIPPER'S TOYBOX

First published 1993 by Hodder and Stoughton Children's Books,
a division of Hodder and Stoughton Ltd.

First U.S. edition 1993

Library of Congress Cataloging-in-Publication Data
Inkpen, Mick.
Kipper's birthday/Mick Inkpen.
p.   cm.
"Gulliver books."
Summary: A delay in delivering the invitations to Kipper the dog's
birthday party causes his friends to come on the wrong day.
ISBN 0-15-200503-X
[1. Birthdays — Fiction. 2. Parties — Fiction. 3. Dogs — Fiction.]
I. Title.
PZ7.I564Kj   1993
[E] — dc20   92-28202

A B C D E

KIPPER'S BIRTHDAY

MICK INKPEN

Gulliver Books
Harcourt Brace Jovanovich, Publishers
San Diego   New York   London
Printed in Italy

It was the day before Kipper's
birthday. He was busy with his
paints making party invitations.
In large letters he painted,

Plees come to my bithday party
tomoro at 12 o cloc dont be lat

He hung them up to dry and
set about making a cake.

Kipper had not made a cake before.
He put some raisins and eggs and
raisins and flour and sugar and
raisins into a bowl. Then he stirred
the mixture until his arm ached.

Next he added some cherries and
stirred it once more. Then he rolled it
with a rolling pin and looked at what
he had made.

"I have made a flat thing,"
he said.

Kipper squeezed the flat thing into a cake shape and watched it bake in the oven. To his surprise it changed itself slowly into a sort of heap, but it smelled good. He put the last remaining cherry on the top for decoration.

By this time the party invitations were dry.

"I'll deliver them tomorrow," yawned Kipper. "It's too late now."

K ipper woke bright and early on
his birthday. His first thought was:
Balloons! We must have balloons!
But as he rushed downstairs another
thought popped into his head:
Invitations!

Kipper ran all the way to his
best friend's house and stuffed the
invitations into Tiger's paws.

"That one's yours. Those are for the
others," he panted. "Can't stop! Balloons!"

When he had gone Tiger opened
the invitation.

Plees come to my bithday party
tomoro at 12 o cloc dont be lat

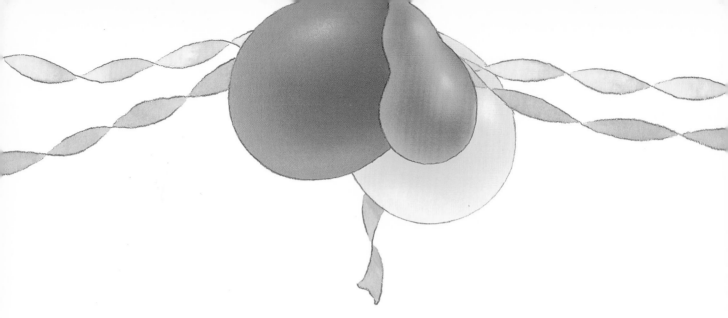

At twelve o'clock Kipper carefully
placed his cake on the table and sat down
to wait for a knock at the door.

He waited. And he waited. But nobody
came. Not even Tiger.

The cake smelled good, and Kipper
began to feel hungry. At one o'clock he
ate the cherry from the top.

Two o'clock passed. Still nobody came. Kipper pulled off a large piece of cake and broke it open to see if there was a cherry inside. There were two. He ate them both and began to feel better.

By five o'clock there were no more cherries to be found.

Kipper stretched out on the table feeling very full and very sleepy.

K ipper slept through the
evening and into the night.
He dreamed that he was
climbing a mountain made of
cake and dodging great cake boulders
as they crashed toward him.

Even when the sun streamed
through his window the next morning
he did not wake, but snored
peacefully until noon
when he was awakened
by a knock at the door.

His friends had come.
"Happy birthday,
Kipper!" said Jake.
"Happy birthday,
Kipper!" said Holly.
"And many happy
returns!" said Tiger.
Kipper blinked
and rubbed his eyes.
"But my birthday
was yesterday," he
said sleepily.

They looked at the invitation.

Plees come to my bithday party tomoro at 12 o cloc dont be lat

Kipper looked puzzled.
"So my birthday is not until tomorrow," he said. "We haven't missed it after all!"

N o, no, no," said Tiger. "Your birthday must have been *tomorrow* the day before yesterday."

Kipper looked puzzled again.

Tiger went on, "So yesterday it would have been *today,* but today it was *yesterday.* Do you see?"

Kipper did not see. His brain was beginning to ache so he said, "Cake anyone?"

And then he remembered that he had eaten it all.

Never mind," said Tiger. "Why don't
you open your presents?"

The presents seemed a bit odd.
The first was a napkin from Jake.
The second was some candles from Holly.

"Very useful," said Kipper, trying not
to look disappointed.

But the third was the most
useful of all . . .

It was a cake!